MARVEL
CAPTAIN AMERICA

AN ORIGIN STORY

Based on the Marvel comic book series **Captain America**
Adapted by **Rich Thomas Jr.**
Illustrated by **Val Semeiks, Bob McLeod,**
Hi-Fi Design, and **The Storybook Art Group**

New York
Los Angeles

SUSTAINABLE FORESTRY INITIATIVE   Certified Sourcing
www.sfiprogram.org
SFI-00993
This Label Applies to Text Stock Only

For Duke
  —RT

© 2014 MARVEL

Published by Marvel Press, an imprint of Disney Book Group. No part of this book may be reproduced or transmitted in any form or by any means, electronic or mechanical, including photocopying, recording, or by any information storage and retrieval system, without written permission from the publisher. For information address Marvel Press, 1101 Flower Street, Glendale, California 91201.

Cover illustrated by Pat Olliffe and Brian Miller
Designed by Jennifer Redding

Printed in the United States of America
Second Edition
13579108642
G942-9090-6-14023
ISBN 978-1-4847-0073-0

Before you were born—in fact, long before
even the oldest person you know had been born—a
peaceful little island sat right off the mainland of
a place that was called different things by all the
different nations of people who lived there.

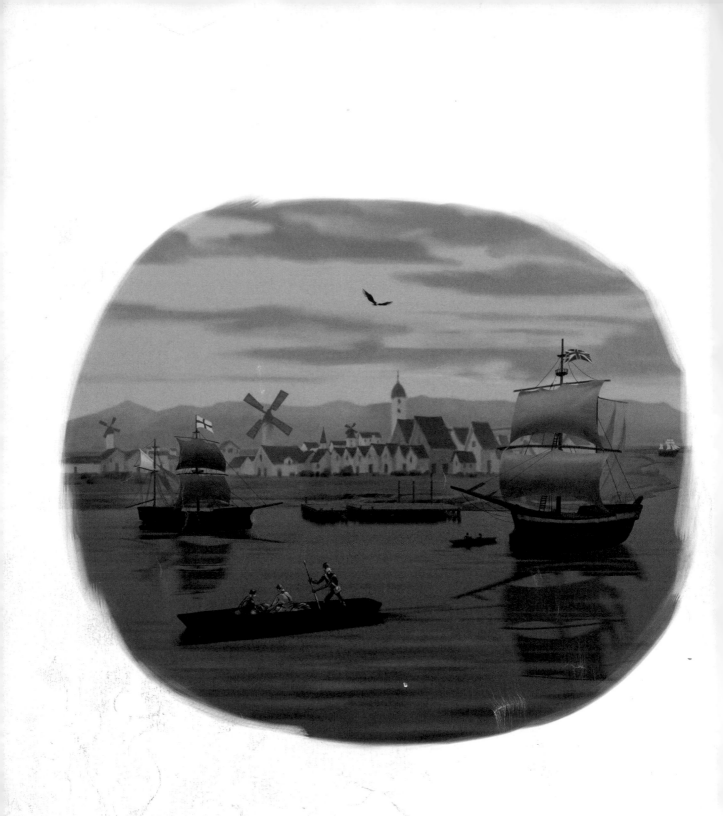

As time went on, more and more
people came to this **little island.**

They wanted to leave behind the lives they led in a place they called the **Old World**

and build new ones in a place where they believed **anything was possible**.

They came from all over the world.

For most, this island was the first stop on the path to a new life in this young nation.

This island was known as Manhattan, in **the city of New York**. The country would be known as the United States of America—or *America*, for short.

Before America was even two hundred years old,

it was called upon to fight alongside other countries in a **terrible war** that was destroying the world.

DAILY BUGLE

WAR!

PEARL HARBOR ATTACKED!

The news of war
moved people.

It seemed like everyone
in the country wanted
to join the army
to **help**.

Including a young man named **Steve Rogers**.

Steve had been upset about the war for some time. Now that America was involved, he could **do something** about it.

Soon, Steve was in a long line of men waiting to be examined. If the men passed, they would be deployed to the war.

Steve waited
his turn.

Every man
so far had
passed.

Steve was
confident
he would, too.

The doctor told Steve that
he was in no shape to join
the army.

But then he told him there was another way to get into the army. He handed Steve a file marked

CLASSIFIED—PROJECT: REBIRTH.

The doctor told Steve that if the experiment worked, he would be able to join the army. Steve said he would try anything to become a soldier. The doctor called in a general named **Chester Phillips**. General Phillips was in charge of Project: Rebirth.

The general led Steve down a **hidden hallway** to a secret exit.

Soon the two men were crossing the bridge into nearby Brooklyn.

They arrived at
an antiques shop
in a run-down,
dangerous-looking
area. An **old woman**
let them in and led
them downstairs.

But the storefront was not an antiques shop at all!
It was a cover for an **underground lab**.

And the owner was not an old
woman, but a **secret agent**!

General Phillips introduced Steve to the project's lead scientist, **Doctor Erskine**.

Erskine told Steve that the **Super-Soldier Serum**...

...combined with the **Vita-Rays**...

. . . would transform him
from frail and sickly. . .

. . . into America's

FIRST AVENGER!

The experiment was a **SUCCESS**!

But before Steve, General Phillips, or anyone else in the lab could notice, an **enemy spy** who had been working in the lab attacked!

He did not want the Americans to have such power!

The doctor was hurt and unable to duplicate the serum.

But Steve, in his new
Super-Soldier body,
was safe.

AND HE WAS ANGRY!

The army put Steve through a very special training camp to teach him how to use his new body.

The general presented Steve with a **special shield** made of the strongest metal known and a **unique costume** to help Steve mask his identity.

With the costume and shield, Steve would now be known as America's most powerful soldier...

CAPTAIN AMERICA!

Captain America's missions were often **dangerous**.

In order to keep his secret safe, the general asked Steve to pretend to be a **clumsy** army private.

But when no one was looking, Steve donned his costume and fought for **justice**.

Steve's reputation as a klutz meant he was transferred often.

But Steve's moving around allowed **Captain America** to fight on many different fronts of the worldwide war!

No one ever suspected that the worst private in the U.S. Army

was also the **best soldier** that the army had.

TANK NO MATCH FOR CAP!

CAP RECEIVES HIGHEST HONOR

Captain America kept on fighting
for **liberty**, until finally...

THE WAR HAD BEEN WON.

Though the country might not always live up to its promises, as long as Steve was able, he vowed to protect it and its ideals: **justice, equality, freedom...**

. . .and the dream of what the nation he loved could accomplish.